The Boxcar Children Mysteries

THE CASTLE MYSTERY

created by
GERTRUDE CHANDLER WARNER

Illustrated by Charles Tang

ALBERT WHITMAN & Company
Morton Grove, Illinois

ISBN 0-8075-1079-3

1 3 5 7 9 10 8 6 4 2

Printed in the U.S.A.

Contents

CHAPTER 1

A Bumpy Ride

A big black car drove through the dark green woods. James Alden turned on the headlights.

"Hmm, I can't see much better," Mr. Alden told Jessie and Henry, his two older grandchildren, who were sitting up front with him. "Guess I'll have to go slower."

"That's okay, Grandfather," said twelve-year-old Jessie.

Wet black branches scraped against the side of the car.

In the backseat, ten-year-old Violet shivered. "I hope it's not too much longer, is it, Grandfather?" she asked.

"No, we're almost there," Grandfather said.

Whenever the road dipped down, a thick fog settled around them. Finally, the car reached a clear stretch of road.

"Look across the lake," Mr. Alden said. "It's awfully misty, but I bet you can spot Drummond Castle."

Six-year-old Benny pressed his nose against the window. "I see something big and gray. I can't tell if it's a rock or a castle."

Fourteen-year-old Henry turned to Benny. "It's a rock *and* a castle. I read in Grandfather's magazine on antiques that Drummond Castle is a smaller copy of a real castle in Germany. Only this one is built on a cliff with a cave underneath!"

"Sounds like a good place for a mystery!" Benny said.

The last Drummond, William Drummond III, had died, and Grandfather's friend, Carrie Bell, had been hired by the Drummond Foundation to turn his magnificent home

into a museum. Knowing how much the Aldens would enjoy visiting a castle, Carrie had invited them to help out.

For some time now, the children had been living with Mr. Alden. He had found his grandchildren staying in a boxcar out in the woods. Now the boxcar was just a cheery playhouse in Mr. Alden's backyard. Henry, Jessie, Violet, and Benny lived in a real house with a proper kitchen and real bedrooms.

The children tried to make out the castle in the distance. They liked staying in new places, especially if they were old places!

For a second, Mr. Alden took his eyes off the road to look at the castle. Just as he was turning back, Henry yelled: "Watch out, Grandfather. There's a car coming! Pull over! Pull over!"

Two bright headlights cut through the fog and raced straight toward the Aldens' car.

"There's no room for it to get by!" Jessie cried out.

Mr. Alden leaned on his horn. He flashed his headlights on and off. The car kept on coming. Finally Grandfather pulled the car into a clearing. The red Jeep raced by as if it were on a two-lane highway, not a narrow, twisty road. The woman at the wheel didn't seem to have any idea that she had almost caused an accident.

Benny and Violet sank back into their seats. They were a little scared, a little tired, and very hungry. It had been a long day.

Their dog, Watch, who was sitting in the backseat, too, let out a sad, hungry cry. Poor Watch had been so good on the long drive. Still, this delay was too much even for a well-behaved dog.

"There, there," Violet crooned. She reached into a bag and gave Watch a dog biscuit.

The treat helped, but the children could see that Watch needed more than a biscuit. He needed a short walk to stretch his legs.

Mr. Alden turned off the engine. "That was a close call. Let's all get a breath of air."

The children opened the car doors. They were glad to sniff the fresh piney breezes. So was Watch, who pulled Violet to this tree and that.

Grandfather handed Jessie his binoculars. "See if you can get these focused for Benny." He pointed across the lake. "Drummond Castle is just past that island. I'm sure Benny would like a better look at the place we'll be staying in, wouldn't you now, Ben?"

"You know I would," Benny answered with a big smile.

Mr. Alden always knew what his youngest grandson liked — castles and caves, mysteries and adventures. When Jessie showed her little brother where to point the binoculars, Benny had a feeling a big adventure was coming up. Through the glasses he could see a tall, gray stone castle with two towers that faced each other.

"Look, look, Henry," Benny handed his older brother the binoculars. "There's even a light shining in one of the towers! Maybe it's a ghost."

"You mean the Drummond family ghost?" Henry joked. "Woooo. Wooo."

Mr. Alden patted Benny's head. "I hate to disappoint you, Benny," he said, "but it's more likely to be Caroline getting your sleeping quarters ready. She said that one of the towers was just the place for four lively children."

"Well, let's get going!" Benny cried. He opened the car door, then whistled for Watch to hop in.

The Aldens didn't mind the rest of the ride around the lake now that the castle was in sight.

Mr. Alden's car climbed and climbed.

"It's like a castle in the air," Jessie said when she looked down at the steep drop off the road.

"Don't look down, whatever you do!" Henry told Benny with a laugh.

Benny, of course, did just that. "Oooo. We're so high up!" he said happily. "Come on, Violet. Open your eyes. It's steep, but it's really pretty. Take a look."

"I . . . I don't think so." Violet kept her eyes shut tight. "Tell me when we're there."

"We're there!" Henry yelled a few minutes later. "You can look now, Violet!"

When Violet's blue eyes fluttered open, she gasped.

Drummond Castle was not at all what she'd expected. Black branches of overgrown vines twisted through the arches of a stone porch. In some places the branches climbed so high, they seemed to strangle the castle. Many of the famous stained glass windows the children had seen in old pictures were boarded up to protect them from damage. The two castle towers disappeared into the fog. The whole place was covered in gloom.

Jessie saw Violet's disappointment. She took her younger sister's hand. "Come on. Let's find Carrie Bell. Grandfather told me she couldn't wait for us to help her fix up this place. It will look much prettier when the fog lifts."

"I guess so," Violet said in a quiet voice. "I do so want to see what a castle looks like, even though it's not a real one. I just wish it looked more like it belonged in a fairy tale instead of a . . . ."

"Scary story!" Benny finished.

CHAPTER 2

A Shadow at the Door

The Aldens unpacked the trunk of the car. Violet kept her eyes on her belongings, not the castle. If only the fog would go away.

But now that they were closer, the castle seemed a little less scary.

Grandfather put his arm around Violet. "You know this castle was built as a home when the first Drummonds came back from their honeymoon in Germany. The first William Drummond built it for his bride — not to keep out armies or dragons."

This made Violet feel a little better. "The stained glass windows make pretty patterns," she noticed.

Jessie and Violet stared at a particularly beautiful round window right over the entrance. "That one is the prettiest," Jessie said. "There's a face painted in the center. See."

"Oh no!" Violet screamed suddenly. "It's a *real* face. Look! Look!"

The Aldens looked up to where Violet was pointing. All they saw was the face of a young knight painted on the central piece of the stained glass.

Violet looked again. "Maybe I'm just a little tired. The fog and mist make everything look so strange."

A beautiful carved stone porch encircled the ground level of the castle. The Aldens went up the steps to ring the bell.

"Try that funny-looking door knocker, Benny," Henry said, giving his brother a boost.

Benny rapped the lion's head door knocker three times.

After the third bang, a huge oak door creaked opened. A long shadow stood there.

"Who're you?" the shadow barked.

The Aldens took a closer look. The shadow was actually a man about Mr. Alden's age but tall, thin, and gruff. The light behind him in the huge hallway had made him seem like a shadow.

Before the Aldens could answer, Carrie Bell came to greet her friends. "Why James, you made it at last!" the smiling older woman said. "I'm sorry you had such a poor day to travel. Our old lake road can be a real challenge in the fog."

"Well, it seems to be clearing now." Mr. Alden turned back to the man. "How do you do, sir? I am James Alden, and these are my grandchildren, Henry, Jessie, Violet, and Benny."

These words seemed to frighten the man. Without saying a thing, he disappeared down a dark hall.

"Oh, Mr. Tooner, come back and meet the Aldens," Carrie called out.

But the man didn't even slow down.

Carrie lowered her voice. "Don't mind poor Mr. Tooner. He's been the caretaker here for many years, just like his father before him. He's very worried about Drummond Castle becoming a museum after it's restored. He does a wonderful job caring for the castle, but he needs help. That's what we're all here for." Carrie turned to Benny. "I heard you make the lion on the door knocker growl, Benny! Now watch this."

Carried gathered the Aldens' umbrellas and stuck them inside the mouth of a ferocious-looking lion statue. "How do you like that?" Carrie asked.

Benny laughed at how silly the lion looked with a mouthful of umbrellas. "He doesn't look nearly so mean now!"

Even Violet had to laugh. She just wished that the big humps of furniture covered with white dust sheets looked as silly as that lion. She half expected some of them to start moving around the room!

Carrie took Violet by the hand. "All the furniture downstairs has been covered up since William Drummond III died last year.

With all of you here to help out, we can make this big old place look homier very soon. Now come upstairs to your rooms."

The Aldens followed Carrie up a winding staircase at the back of the castle. "I know this musty old place looks a bit gloomy today, but you children have a wonderful experience ahead of you. There are so many imaginative objects here like that silly door knocker and the umbrella stand. This castle is full of surprises."

Carrie led the Aldens down a hall off the first landing. She pushed open a heavy wooden door. "This will be your room, James."

Inside the huge room was a canopy bed and a fireplace, tall enough to stand in. Over in the corner stood a suit of armor.

Carrie lifted up Benny. "Raise the front of this armor headpiece." she said.

Benny moved the metal flap, and gasped. Then he laughed. "Somebody put a picture of a boy's face under the helmet!" he told everyone.

Sure enough, a faded drawing of a smiling

boy about Benny's age peeked out from under the armor headpiece.

"I knew you'd like that!" Carrie said. "I think the first Mr. Drummond put it in there as a joke for his boys. He tried to liven up Drummond Castle with some of the furnishings. There are quite a few playful touches all around the castle. You'll see."

"I hope there are some funny things in our rooms. Can we go see them now?" Benny asked.

The children and Watch climbed some more narrow stairs. At the top of the tower were two bright little rooms with windows all around.

"Oh," Violet breathed. The first rays of sunlight they'd seen all day poured into the rooms. "It is so pretty up here." She sounded relieved. "Why there's even a fancy dog bed for Watch. Here Watch!"

Watch liked the dog bed very much. He curled himself up on the red velvet cushion and promptly fell asleep.

"All he needs is a gold crown on his head!" Jessie laughed.

Carrie laughed, too. "The first Drummond family designed this tower and all the furniture in it for their children. As you can see, they didn't forget the family dog either. Here's your bed, Benny. You might have to wear a crown, too!"

Benny bounced himself on a bed with a wonderful headboard of carved animals. The matching bed next to it was for Henry.

"I like these fancy wardrobes," Jessie called out from the room the girls would be using. "There are drawers and shelves for every little thing."

"These are the nicest rooms in the castle," Carrie told the children. "I'm very glad you like them. Sometimes I bring some of my paperwork up here because of the view. The sunlight is always changing."

"It sure is," Benny said. "When we were driving to the castle a light was shining in that other tower across the way. Now it's in this one. Are there bedrooms in that tower, too?"

Carrie shook her head. "Why, no. The people at the Drummond Foundation said that the other tower is always closed off. I gather it suffered damage many years ago."

"But I saw a light up there through Grandfather's binoculars," Benny insisted. "Grandfather says I have sharp eyes."

"I'm sure you do, Benny," Carrie said with a smile. "But the sunlight plays funny tricks up this high, especially with the fog. Maybe you were looking at these rooms while I was getting them ready."

Benny scratched his head. "I don't think so."

Carrie gave Benny a little pat on the shoulder. "Well, this castle even fools me sometimes, and I've been here two weeks. I'm forever finding things that seem to be one thing, then they're another."

After Carrie left, the children unpacked their bags. They put their clothes away in the tidy wardrobe compartments. But the whole time Benny Alden was thinking about the light across the way. He had seen it there, he just knew he had.

CHAPTER 3

A Light Goes on Again

Benny Alden wasn't much for watching sunsets. And he wasn't one for taking naps, either, like Watch. No, Benny Alden was busy waiting for dinner. He stood at the top of the spiral staircase. He stared down as long as he could without getting dizzy.

"I wish we didn't have to wait until tomorrow to go exploring," he said.

Jessie laughed. "Poor Benny. It's too bad it's so late now. Carrie said they only keep a few lights on at night to save on electricity.

Maybe we can take a walk outside after dinner now that the weather has cleared up."

"And see the cave?" Benny asked hopefully.

"Maybe," Jessie answered.

Finally the children heard a bell clang way downstairs.

Henry caught up with Benny, who had hurried ahead. "Living in a castle makes me hungry."

"So does living in a house or a boxcar or a boat," Henry teased.

They were halfway downstairs when Violet remembered something. "I need my sweater — castles are chilly places," she said.

Violet headed back to her room. Castles were scary places, too, she thought. The top of the stairs looked awfully dark. Violet scolded herself. "If I'm going to be staying in a castle, I had better get used to it. I will just watch my feet. Then I won't notice the dark so much."

The sunset was almost over when Violet got to her room. She couldn't help looking at the beautiful evening sky. That's when she noticed the light in the tower across the way.

Violet got her grandfather's binoculars and tried to focus them. She caught a blurry glimpse of a man — or a woman? — with short, dark hair. Just when she got the lenses focused, the tower light went off.

Violet put down the binoculars. She grabbed her sweater and raced downstairs to the castle kitchen.

"There you both are!" Carrie said to Violet and a young woman who had just come into the kitchen, too. Like Violet, the woman was out of breath.

Carrie stood over a pot of steaming soup. "Take a seat anywhere." Turning to the woman, Carrie said, "Sandy, these new visitors are the Aldens." To the Aldens she added, "Please meet Sandy Munson, my new assistant."

Grandfather, Henry, Jessie, and Benny stood up to say hello. The other two people at the table did not. A young man kept right on sipping his soup, and Mr. Tooner just stared for a long time at the young woman.

His stare gave Violet the shivers.

"Here you go, Sandy," Carrie said, handing her some soup. "Why are you out of breath? I thought I heard the Jeep pull in quite a while ago."

Henry and Jessie looked at each other. Henry knew that Jessie was thinking the same thing he was. Sandy was the woman who'd almost run them off the road earlier that day.

The woman brushed back her short brown bangs nervously. "Uh, no. No, I just drove in from town."

"Well, there are always so many strange sounds around Drummond Castle," Carrie said. "Who knows what they are? Now you and Violet sit next to each other."

Violet tried to talk to Sandy. "By any chance is your room across from ours in the other tower?"

The young woman's hand shook, and she nearly spilled her soup. "Of course not! My room is down on this floor. No one uses the other tower. It's been closed up since Mr. Drummond died. It's off limits!"

"Now, now," Carrie said. "I told Violet and the other children what funny tricks the sunlight plays on the castle. The sunset sometimes reflects off the towers."

"I don't think so, Carrie. You see, the sun had already gone down," Violet explained. "I'm sure there was a real light on in the tower. Then it disappeared."

"Impossible," said Sandy.

"Well, let's make this food disappear." Carrie said, trying to smooth things over at the table. "Oh, and you haven't met Tom Brady, yet, Violet. Tom knows everything there is to know about antiques, rare books, paintings, and musical instruments."

Violet nodded to the young man seated next to Mr. Tooner.

"Violet plays a musical instrument," Jessie said proudly. "The violin."

Mr. Tooner's hand shook so much he dropped his knife. After picking it up, he left the table without a word.

"I'm sorry," Jessie said. "Did I say something wrong?"

Carrie shook her head sadly. "Well, you

probably don't know about the Drummond violin. It's been missing since William Drummond III died. Mr. Tooner thinks everyone believes that he's the one who lost it."

"Or took it," Sandy Munson broke in. "After all, he *was* the only one living here after Mr. Drummond passed away."

Tom Brady looked at Carrie. "There is no denying what Sandy says. That violin disappeared while Mr. Tooner was working here."

"Please," Carrie began. "Let's not get into this discussion again. We don't know whether it was lost or whether William Drummond hid it for safekeeping before he died. We truly do not know."

The Aldens could see that neither Sandy nor Tom accepted what Carrie said.

"We simply must begin to work together," Carrie said calmly. "There is no other way. I do believe that violin will turn up as we do our work. Why, already I've found a few treasures while getting some of the rooms in order."

Tom Brady listened to Carrie's speech. He

did not look one bit happy about working together with anyone. "Well," he announced, "my work is very special. Not just anyone should go rummaging through antiques, let alone help fix them."

Carrie cut him off. "We will organize everything in the morning. The Aldens are good, careful workers. I'm quite sure there is plenty they can do. Maybe tomorrow they can start out with you, Sandy."

"You mean I have to baby-sit?" Sandy complained. "When there's so much real work to do?"

"There are no babies in our family, Miss Munson," Mr. Alden said. "Just hardworking children who know what to do with tools, paint brushes, or a needle and thread. As for me, I noticed that those vines over the stonework porch could use a good pruning. They need to be cut back before any more water seeps into the cracks. We Aldens are ready to go."

Mr. Alden's little speech seemed to upset Tom and Sandy. They didn't look up from their plates again until they heard Carrie mention Violet's interest in the violin.

"Well, it would be lovely to have you children find the Stradivarius while you're here," Carrie said to Violet. "Maybe you could play it."

Sandy's face suddenly lit up. "Oh, yes, I would love to hear it played again."

Carrie looked surprised. "Whatever do you mean, Sandy?"

Sandy pushed herself away from the table. "Just that I . . . uh I . . . like violin music, too. That's all I meant. Now I'd better finish unloading the Jeep."

"That's odd," Carrie said. "This is the third time Sandy has mentioned wanting to hear the Stradivarius again. I'm sure she's never heard such an instrument even once."

"A Stradivarius," Violet breathed. "My violin teacher told me how wonderful they sound."

"Did your violin teacher tell you how valuable they are?" Tom asked in an unfriendly voice. "Not that a child could ever play such an instrument. Even famous musicians are lucky to get their hands on one."

"Tom is correct about that," Carrie said. "It's sad that such a treasure is missing."

The word "treasure" perked up Benny right away. "Why do you think the Stradi . . . Stradi . . . whatever it's called is in this castle? Maybe Mr. Drummond sold it and didn't tell anyone."

"Nonsense!" Tom Brady said loudly. "He kept track of that violin like his own child. He saved every clipping about the auction where he bought it and careful records about when he lent it out to well-known musicians. I'm an expert in rare instruments myself. I can tell you that the Drummond Stradivarius has never shown up."

When Tom and Grandfather went upstairs, the children stayed and helped Carrie clean up.

"Why does Tom talk in such an angry voice?" Benny asked.

Carrie sighed. "He was upset when the Drummond Foundation hired me to coordinate the castle restoration. They hired Tom first. But the trustees put me in charge when he refused to work with anyone else.

He is an expert on old things. But you can see we need more than that. We need several people who can work together."

Benny could not understand this. "Why can't everybody work together? That's what we do! See, the dishes are done already!"

Carrie Bell smiled. "That's what I mean. It's just taking Tom awhile to get the idea. I also have to train Sandy Munson. She's been here a week. I need to teach her to take care with her work and slow down."

"We know," Jessie said. "She almost ran Grandfather off the road today in her Jeep. I don't think she even saw our car."

Carrie shook her head. "I've had to warn her several times about being careful on the lake road. She's just too quick. She is always jumping ahead of herself. She begins a job in one room, then I find her in another. She is never where she is supposed to be."

"How did Sandy get the job as your assistant?" Jessie asked.

"The Drummond Foundation told me she had done a great deal of research on Drummond Castle," Carrie explained. "I must admit that from her first day here she knew where things were. I believe she will be a good worker. If we can only get her to stay with one job at a time! Maybe you children can show her the patient way to do things."

Henry could see that Benny wasn't looking too patient himself. "Do you need us for anything else tonight?" Henry asked. "We'd like to take a walk around the castle if that's okay with you."

Carrie smiled at the children. "Why, of course. I keep several flashlights by the kitchen door here." Carrie clicked on a light switch. "This spotlight will help you see where you're going."

The children stepped outside. The fog was completely gone. A big silvery moon was rising over the lake.

"Now it looks like a fairy tale castle," Violet whispered.

The children walked with Watch out to the cliff.

"Not too close, Benny," Jessie warned.

"I know, I know," Benny answered. "Grandfather told me about not going near

the edge of a cliff that time we climbed Old
Flat Top. He said a boy should be told a
thing only once, and he was right!"

Jessie laughed. "Then I won't have to tell
you again."

The cool night air soon reminded the children of their cozy beds up in the tower. Violet pulled her sweater tighter against the
whistling wind.

When the children went to explore the side
of the castle, the wind off the lake died down.
That's when everyone realized there was another sound in the air.

"Listen," Violet whispered. "It's a violin.
It's playing a pretty piece called 'Redbird.' I
know that tune!"

Henry pointed his flashlight in the direction of the music. There was nothing but
blackness where the sound was coming from.
"The music sounds as if it's coming from the
cliff. That's very strange."

"A lot of things about this castle are
strange, Henry," Violet said in a worried
voice. "When I went back for my sweater
tonight, I saw a light coming from the other

tower that is supposed to be locked. And it wasn't the sunset. I also heard footsteps coming from that direction right before Sandy Munson came down into the kitchen."

Henry shone his flashlight in different directions. "We need to explore the castle when it's light out. I'd like to check that footpath over there. See?"

The children followed the flashlight beam to where the cliff seemed to dip down.

Benny looked over, but all he could see was blackness. "Maybe that's how we get to the caves," Benny said. "Can we go looking tomorrow, Henry? Can we?"

"Sure thing, Benny," Henry answered. "Now let's head back. Careful where you walk."

The ground was slippery on the way back to the castle. The children watched every step they took so they wouldn't fall. Had they looked up just then, they might have seen one more odd thing. Up in the tower someone else was watching their every step, too.

CHAPTER 4

Someone Listens In

"Bless you!" "Bless you!" voices said all morning long. Benny was down on his knees cleaning the carved wooden legs of the dining-room table with a soft toothbrush. Jessie was making a list in an old ledger. And Violet was dusting glass and china figurines. All morning long the dust made everyone sneeze. Meanwhile Grandfather and Henry were working outside.

"Careful! Watch that!" Sandy said every time one of the Aldens pulled something delicate from the huge built-in china closet.

The Aldens didn't need Sandy Munson to tell them to take care. No one was better at handling fragile things than they were.

"Don't worry. We'll be careful," Jessie said. She remembered Grandfather Alden's advice. Find out what new people like to do, and you'll make a friend. That's just what she was going to do with Sandy Munson.

"How did you learn so much about Drummond Castle?" Jessie began in her friendliest voice. "You seem to know your way around this big place so well after such a short time."

"What do you mean by that?" Sandy demanded.

"I'm sorry," Jessie apologized. "I only meant . . ." Jessie stopped before she got into any more trouble with Sandy.

Sandy pointed to a low cabinet. "Hand me that box, please," she ordered Benny. "It's heavy, so watch out."

Benny carefully pulled down a large leather-covered box. "Whew, what's in here?" The box *was* heavy!

"Silverware!" Sandy snapped. "Now be careful!"

Benny was as careful as could be. He held the heavy box in his arms for Sandy to take. Yet she grabbed it so fast that it crashed to the floor. Silverware scattered all over.

"Now look what happened!" Sandy yelled. "Please leave the rest of the work in here. I'll finish up by myself."

Benny Alden wasn't used to sharp voices. He bit his lip. "I'm sorry," he apologized.

Sandy took the ledger from Jessie. "I'll do the rest." Jessie, Violet, and Benny left the dining room quietly.

"Come on," Jessie said. "Carrie said we should take our lunch down to the lake after we finished in the dining room. I guess Sandy thinks we're finished."

"A picnic would be nice," Violet said softly. "That was a dusty job."

The children went to their rooms for their jackets and came back down the narrow twisty staircase.

"Look," Benny whispered when the children reached the second-floor landing. "Grandfather must be finished with his work, too. His door's open."

But when they entered his room, they got a surprise. Mr. Tooner was in Mr. Alden's room, kneeling on the floor. He was trying to pry up some floorboards underneath the carpet.

Benny felt his nose twitch. "Aaaachoo!" he cried when he couldn't keep from sneezing.

Startled, Mr. Tooner turned around. "What are you kids doing here?"

Jessie stepped forward. "We came to visit our grandfather."

Mr. Tooner banged in the floorboard with his hammer. "Well, you can see he's not here. He and that boy have been out on the porch trying to destroy that wisteria vine that's older than the two of 'em put together! That's where they are. Hmph!"

Violet was a quiet one but not when it came to her family. "My grandfather is a wonderful gardener. Why he even had a rose named after him! He would never destroy any living thing!"

Mr. Tooner looked as if he was about to apologize, but he changed his mind.

"Well, if I didn't always have to be fixing things for all the guests that keep coming here, then maybe I could have trimmed that vine myself. Now scat!"

Jessie took Benny's hand, then Violet's, and the three went down to the kitchen. "I just wish people around here would let us help more," Jessie said to Carrie.

"Help?" Carrie said. "Why you children are just in time to help me with this platter of sandwiches."

Jessie helped Carrie put sandwiches on a big tray. "Sorry we're so early for lunch, but Sandy told us to leave for now. She wants to finish the work in the dining room by herself."

Carrie shook her head. "Dear, dear. I wish she wouldn't. She means well, but she can be all thumbs around delicate things. She doesn't listen. Well, I'd better get up there before there's a crash. I know you children can fix yourselves a little picnic together, now can't you?"

"We sure can!" Benny said. "Picnics are one thing we're good at."

After they'd gathered some lunch, the children stopped by to see how Henry and Grandfather were doing.

"The castle looks brighter already," Violet said when she saw how many vines had been cut back.

Grandfather and Henry stood back to check their work.

"I'd like to be here in two months when this starts blooming," Mr. Alden said. "Who votes for another trip to Drummond Castle in the summer?"

Mr. Alden was surprised that only Henry raised his hand.

"What is it, Jessie?" Henry asked. "Don't you like working at Drummond Castle?"

Jessie nodded. "We would like working here if anyone besides Carrie would let us. Sandy thinks we're going to break things. This morning Tom wouldn't even let Violet take a peek at the beautiful books he discovered in the library."

"And Mr. Tooner thinks we're pests!" Benny said, his eyes full of surprise and hurt. "He shooed us out of your room when he was fixing broken floorboards."

Now it was Mr. Alden's turn to look surprised. "Broken floorboards! Why the floors in that room are as solid as rock. Caroline said it's one of the few rooms that doesn't need any renovation at all. I can't imagine what Mr. Tooner was doing in there."

"Chasing us out!" Benny said hotly.

After the children gave Mr. Alden some sandwiches, they took the steep footpath down to the lake. No one was going to stop them from having a picnic!

"Look at the pretty view," Jessie said halfway down. "I can see why the Drummonds picked this spot to build their castle. It's perfect."

Indeed it was. Out in front lay a sparkling lake. Behind the children was a wall of rock and moss that would soon be full of delicate wildflowers.

"Carrie told me the first Mr. Drummond put in this railing and these steps so his children would have a shortcut to the beach," Henry mentioned. "She said to look for a gate halfway down. The Drummonds in-

stalled it after one of their children got lost in the cave."

"Well I'd like to get lost in there, too," Benny said when they passed by a gate that blocked a cave entrance. "Wooo. Wooo."

"*Wooo. Wooo,*" his echo said back.

"Do you suppose the violin could be hidden in there?" Violet asked, remembering the music they had heard on their walk the night before.

Henry shook his head. "I don't think so. It's too damp to keep a valuable instrument in there. And look how rusty that lock is. Carrie said the gate has been locked since way before William Drummond died."

Benny rattled the gate. "I sure wish there was another way to get in here."

"I can't decide whether to eat, or hike, or hike *and* eat," Jessie said when the children reached the little lake beach.

"It's too cold for a hike," Benny said, "so let's eat."

That settled it. The children went on down to the lake. They set their picnic lunch on a flattened tree trunk lying in the sand.

Benny got busy making sand chairs all around the log so they could eat at a proper table.

"This should be a restaurant when they turn the castle into a museum," Benny said proudly.

"Or a tea shop," Violet added.

"Or a snack bar." Jessie handed out thick sandwiches made from Carrie's leftover roast chicken.

When Henry finished eating, he stood up to stretch out. "Pruning is hard work. It looks so easy, but to do it right takes a long time. My arm muscles ache. From down here I can see that Grandfather and I still have plenty left to do. Look."

Jessie looked up at the castle. For the first time, she noticed a small building set into the cliff. "Never mind the castle, Henry. Look there."

All the children looked up to where Jessie was pointing. A pretty little stone house was built right into the side of a cliff.

"It's almost like those Indian dwellings we saw out West," Violet said. "Only this one is like a cottage. I wish we could go see it."

"That must be Mr. Tooner's cottage," Jessie explained. "From what Carrie said, I thought it was attached to the castle. But it's all by itself."

"And so is Mr. Tooner," Violet said.

A cold wind began to blow across the lake. The picnic was over. Even Benny was ready to get back to work. On the return trip up the footpath, he went right by the cave entrance. He didn't even stop to make an echo.

Carrie was waiting in the kitchen with a clipboard. "I hope you've had fun. This afternoon we're going to tackle the great hall. The Drummonds held banquets and dances in there," Carrie told the children. "Now the room isn't used, but somebody . . . well, I'd like to see it filled with guests again. But first we need to fix it up."

Violet wasn't keen on this plan. The great hall was full of big white shapes that looked like ghost chairs and ghost tables. She didn't even like to walk by that room. In fact, when she walked in, Violet thought she saw a sheet-covered chair move.

A minute later, she felt very silly when Carrie began to pull back the draperies and open the windows for fresh air. The room began to look more normal. Carrie removed the dust sheets from a few pieces of furniture.

"Now look at this beautiful sofa," Carrie said. "Try it out, Benny. You too, Violet."

Violet and Benny sat themselves on opposite sides of a fancy S-shaped curved sofa. The seats were placed so that the two Aldens were nearly face to face.

"It's called a conversational sofa. This is how young ladies and gentlemen socialized in the old days," Carrie said. "Between dances a young lady and a young man might chat with each other while sitting on this sofa."

With that, Benny bolted from the funny-shaped sofa. No one would catch him talking to a girl at a dance!

Henry came in with a box of cleaning supplies.

Carrie looked around the room. "You know, I think for this afternoon, we should just work on polishing up the woodwork.

Let's leave the rest of the dust cloths on the furniture for now."

The children set to work. The boys began on the wood trim around the windows and doorways. Henry was tall and could polish the high door frames and the tops of the cabinets. Benny was just the right height to reach down and dust off everything that was low.

Carrie and the girls rolled up their sleeves. They removed the dust covers from two large oak tables and several small tables. There was plenty to do.

When the afternoon light began to fade, Carrie put down her polishing rag. "Whew, we got quite a bit done. We can finish in here tomorrow."

"And maybe we can clean those tall windows," Jessie added. "This room would be much brighter if the windows weren't so dusty."

"That sounds like a good plan, Jessie," Carrie said. "Now I want you children to take the rest of the afternoon off. You've done plenty of work for one day."

Benny put down the feather duster. "Do you think we could start looking for the violin in here, Carrie?"

Carrie smiled. "I don't see why not! Of course, Mr. Tooner said he made a complete search of every nook and cranny in the castle. But the poor man has so much else to do, I can't imagine he checked everywhere."

"I hope not," Benny said. "I mean to find that violin myself!"

Benny Alden didn't waste any time. He opened every cabinet and looked inside every bookcase. He gently tugged on each painting. Maybe there was a secret safe hidden behind one of them!

"Nuts!" he said when he was almost through. "There are no good hiding places in here, Carrie."

But Benny was wrong. There was at least one very good hiding place in the great hall. Under a dust sheet covering a big chair, which Benny hadn't thought to check, sat someone who had been listening to every word.

CHAPTER 5

Something Lost, Something Found

At breakfast the next morning, everyone met with Carrie to plan the day's work. She was pleased at how quickly jobs got done with the Aldens' help. Still, it took some coaxing to get everybody to work together.

"I'm sending Sandy to town. We're very low on groceries," Carrie announced. "Who else would like to go?"

No one spoke up. Mr. Tooner stared at Sandy in that odd way he had. Tom kept on scribbling something in his notebook. As for the Aldens, they were full of other plans.

"It's such a fine day," Mr. Alden said, "I'm going to do some clean-up work on the grounds."

"Jessie, Violet, and I are going to tackle those big windows in the great hall," Henry told Carrie.

"What about you, Benny?" Carrie asked.

"I'm going to search for the violin! I'll finish looking in the great hall. If it's not there, I'm going to search the castle high and low!"

This got everyone's attention right away.

First, Sandy spoke up. "Maybe Benny should come shopping with me after all. I . . . uh . . . I mean, there's so much to carry."

Mr. Tooner, who never said much, asked for Benny's help, too. "Well, I could use a boy to hammer a few things."

Even Tom needed Benny all of a sudden. He put down his pen next to his notebook. "I'll put you to work. Why don't you box up some of the books in the great hall so I can catalogue them? I'll put a carton in there right now." With that, Tom rushed upstairs.

Benny didn't know what to say. Why did

everyone need him just when he wanted to explore the castle? He stopped eating his pancakes and looked up at Carrie.

"There seems to be a great demand for a hardworking boy like you!" Carrie said with an encouraging smile. "But don't worry. There aren't too many books left in the great room. You'll still have plenty of time to explore afterwards."

Before Sandy went out, she said to Benny: "Well, as long as you're poking around, see if you can find the charm bracelet I lost the other day. I think it must be in the dining hall."

"Okay," Benny agreed, though that wouldn't be nearly as exciting as finding a valuable violin.

After Mr. Tooner and Mr. Alden left, Carrie and the children tidied up the kitchen.

"Well, I'm glad everyone has a job," Carrie said. "And I'm glad Sandy won't be underfoot. I keep finding her here, there, and everywhere."

"Well, today *I'm* going to be here, there, and everywhere," Benny said with a smile.

The children gathered up some buckets, sponges, rags, and cleaning supplies.

"Henry, why don't you put everything in the dumbwaiter, and we can send it up to the first floor?" Carrie asked. "I don't like carrying a lot of things on the narrow back stairs."

Henry opened the doors to the dumbwaiter. The children could hear a man's voice traveling down the passageway: ". . . just figured out how to stop all this snooping around. But I need to know if you have a buyer."

The voice faded out before the children heard anything else.

"Whose voice is that?" Jessie asked.

Henry thought. "I'm not sure if it's Tom or Mr. Tooner. Probably Tom, since he talks to a lot of antiques dealers."

There was so much to do, no one had time to puzzle out who or what they had overheard. The children stacked their cleaning supplies inside the dumbwaiter. Benny pulled the rope to send it upstairs.

In the great hall, everyone had a job to

do. First, Henry took down the heavy velvet draperies.

"I'll take them outside and hang them," Carrie said. "There's a stiff breeze coming off the lake. That will blow some of the dust from these old curtains."

Violet helped Jessie remove the dust sheets from the rest of the furniture. "Goodness, look at this!" Violet cried, pulling a sheet off a big chair. She held up Sandy's missing charm bracelet.

"Why would Sandy's bracelet be in this chair?" Benny wondered.

"Most of this furniture has been covered up since we arrived," Henry pointed out. "There are some strange things going on in this old castle," Jessie said.

Violet's face was pale. "Ever since we got here, I don't like going by the rooms where the furniture is covered up. If there's a breeze blowing or anything, the sheets move and . . . I don't know. I sometimes have the feeling someone is hiding under them."

Benny looked up at Violet. "Me, too!"

Henry could tell that Benny and Violet

were still a little nervous. He pulled a dust sheet off the last piece of furniture. "There, now it looks pretty normal in here, doesn't it?"

"Normal for an old castle," Violet said. She felt a little better now that everything was uncovered.

Benny felt better too. He settled himself down to work in front of a bookcase. Carrie had been right. There weren't too many books left to pack up for Tom. In fact, Benny wondered why Tom even needed him for such a simple job.

"Look!" Benny said. "Here are some albums with pictures of the castle a long time ago."

Benny got the boring work out of the way quickly. He dusted off old books and boxed them. Then he picked up a big green leather photo album. Inside were old black-and-white photos taken around Drummond Castle. There were some boys his very own age on ponies in front of the castle stable. There was a beautiful greenhouse with a wedding party posed in front of it.

Then, in one photo, Benny saw a familiar face. "Come here," he called out to Henry and his sisters. "Doesn't this look like Mr. Tooner?" He pointed to a thin young man with a serious look on his face.

"I think it is," Jessie said. "And, look, he's holding a violin in the picture. There seems to be some kind of square dance out in the stables."

Violet took a look. "I don't think that could be the Stradivarius — not at a country dance."

"Aw, shucks," Benny said. "Why not?"

"Sorry, Benny," Violet said. "This looks like a fine fiddle Mr. Tooner is holding, but he's playing with other country musicians in this picture. They wouldn't use rare instruments."

"Nuts!" Benny said.

Jessie wanted to cheer up Benny. "Well, there is a clue in the picture staring right at you."

"What is it, Jessie? Tell me. Please," Benny begged.

"It's Mr. Tooner, of course. Now we know

that he plays the violin. Maybe he's the one we have heard playing."

"I still wish this was the violin everybody is looking for," Benny said. "Maybe I'll find an even better clue."

Benny didn't have to wait long for a better clue. In fact, he was holding one right in his hands. "What does this paper say, Jessie? It fell out of one of the books Tom told me to pack. I can read print but not handwriting. Can you read it to me?"

Jessie took a look at the paper Benny was holding. "Hmm. I'm not sure what this is, some sort of map. I guess we should have Carrie take a look at it."

The other children looked over Jessie's shoulder as she turned the map this way and that.

"It looks like someone was trying to scribble down directions," Henry said when he studied the paper.

"Directions to what?" Benny wanted to know.

"I can't figure it out," Henry said. "Maybe it's nothing much. But why don't we try to

match up some of the places on this map?"

"Hooray!" Benny said. "I like following maps."

With an adventure ahead of them, the Aldens finished their work in no time. Soon the windows of the great room sparkled. And Benny had a box of books for Tom when he came in to get them.

"Still here, I see." As usual Tom had an annoyed look on his face when he spoke to the children.

"We were careful with all these old things," Jessie explained. "Benny was especially careful with the books you wanted."

"Fine, fine," Tom said. "Well, move along then. I have work to finish in here myself. Carrie said to tell you to take the rest of the morning off if you're finished. So you can leave now."

"That's what we were about to do," Violet said. "We just need to help Jessie and Henry gather up the window-washing things."

Tom seemed to want the room to himself. He shifted from one foot to the other until the children finally left.

Carrie was sitting at the kitchen table going through old papers when the children returned there.

"Look what Violet found!" Benny flashed Sandy's charm bracelet in front of Carrie. "It was on one of the chairs that was covered up."

Carrie sighed. "Ah, that Sandy. She's always leaving things around. She starts a job, then next thing I know she begins something else. I really wish the foundation had sent someone over who was already trained. Or that there were more Aldens to go around!"

"Don't tell that to Tom Brady," Henry said as he dumped the water bucket into the sink. "He seems to think there are already too many Aldens. He couldn't wait to shoo us out of the great hall."

"He didn't give Benny so much as a thank-you for packing up all those books for him," Jessie said.

Carrie got up from her work to give Benny a big squeeze. "Well, here's a hug *and* a thank-you, Benny," Carrie said. "I guess Tom just likes to be by himself. I'm sure he appreciates what you did. I find that many people who work with old things like to work alone. I suppose Tom enjoys browsing through all the books he finds to see what treasures they might hold."

Benny waved the paper they had found in one of the books. "Here's a treasure we found in an old book. It's a map, and we're going to see where it goes."

Carrie checked the paper to see if it was old or valuable. "I bet that's something William Drummond drew up for his children. Like that drawing inside the suit of armor. He was always sending his children on treasure hunts. So go ahead," Carrie said cheerfully. "But save the paper. I doubt it's valuable, but when you're finished with it I'll file it away with some of the other personal papers I've found. That looks like a morning's adventure."

"I sure hope so!" Benny cried.

CHAPTER 6

Benny Finds Two Treasures

Mr. Alden was out on the grounds when his grandchildren spotted him. They couldn't wait to tell their grandfather about the map.

Watch dashed over from the garden to greet the children.

"Watch has been whining for you children to come outdoors all morning." Mr. Alden called out. "I'm afraid he finds gardening rather dull. You probably have something far more exciting for him."

"We sure do, Grandfather," Benny said.

58

"We found a map in an old book. We're going on a treasure hunt. The greenhouse is where it starts."

"That's right over there," Grandfather pointed. "Only it's not really a greenhouse anymore but the skeleton of one."

The children went inside the empty framework. Anyone could see there wasn't anything hidden or secret about where they were standing.

"Let's go to the next place on the map," Benny suggested.

"That's the stable we saw in the picture," Jessie said. "Let's take a look."

The children skipped over to an old building not far from the greenhouse. There were several empty horse stalls inside, but that was all.

Benny's face fell.

"Let's walk back and forth to see if the floor sounds hollow any place," Henry suggested when he saw Benny's disappointment. "You never know. There might be a secret passage that leads someplace."

The children walked in small steps. If

there was a secret trap door they were going to find it. Benny walked up and down the length of the stable. There was nothing.

"Come on, buddy," Henry said. "Let's go to the next place on the map."

Jessie began to wonder if the map was not a treasure map at all. She felt sorry for Benny. She knew he was counting on an adventure today. That's when she got one of her good ideas.

"We'll make our own treasure hunt," Jessie told Benny. "Violet and I will run ahead and hide some treats for you and Henry to find. Meet us back here in about twenty minutes. We'll give you back the map, and you and Henry can follow it. What do you think of that?"

"I think the treasures should be something to eat!" Benny suggested. "We couldn't eat that old violin anyway."

While they waited, Henry and Benny decided to see what Grandfather was doing. When they returned to the garden they were surprised to see him with Mr. Tooner.

"Is your treasure hunt over already,

boys?" Mr. Alden asked. "I don't see you carrying a bag of gold! Well, come see how a professional gardener does things. Do you mind, Mr. Tooner?"

Mr. Tooner went about his work without greeting the boys. "Now the first thing you do with a lilac bush is you look for the old wood," he said gruffly. "That's what you cut — like this." Mr. Tooner snapped off a branch with his pruning scissors.

"Henry, why don't you give it a try?" Mr. Alden suggested.

Henry took the scissors from Mr. Tooner and started to cut.

"Nope. Not that high, my boy. Cut it right down to the ground," Mr. Tooner explained. "That's the way."

Mr. Tooner supervised the boys as they took turns. "Now you don't want to hack a growing thing like this the way some people do. You cut some of the old growth — not all of it, mind you — to make way for the new. Now you folks can do the rest."

Mr. Alden and his grandsons watched Mr. Tooner slowly walk back to the castle.

"Well, boys, I'm glad you came along when you did," Mr. Alden said. "There's nothing I like better than learning something new from a fine gardener."

"I thought I didn't like Mr. Tooner, but now I do," Benny announced.

"I couldn't agree more," Mr. Alden said. "I noticed Mr. Tooner always seemed to be around wherever I looked. So I asked him to show me a few things. That's often a good way to make friends with a stranger."

Henry pruned some of the other lilac branches. "Did Mr. Tooner talk about Drummond Castle?"

"Just how to properly prune these lilacs," Mr. Alden said. "Mr. Tooner makes every word count. Not much for chitchat and such. But that's fine with me. I told him we were only here to help out, and he could teach us how to do what needs doing."

"I'm glad to know Mr. Tooner is such a good teacher, Grandfather," Henry said. "I wish he would show me how to play a tune on the fiddle."

Mr. Aldren looked puzzled. Benny explained. "We found a picture of Mr. Tooner at a dance a long time ago. He was holding a fiddle. We think we heard him practicing the other night."

"That wouldn't surprise me a bit," Mr. Alden said. "He's got fine hands for it. Now where are Jessie and Violet? I think Benny's had enough of gardening."

"And not enough of treasure hunting," Benny agreed. "It seems longer than twenty minutes."

Henry checked his watch. "It *is* longer than twenty minutes. Let's go back to the castle and see what's holding them up."

Violet and Jessie were nowhere around when the boys went to the castle. Carrie said the girls had come in to get a bag of hard candy and two flashlights, and had then run off again.

"Here's a flashlight for you boys," Carrie said.

Benny took the flashlight from Carrie. "Where were the girls going that they might need one?" he asked.

"Let's check upstairs," Henry suggested.

"They might still be here getting their jackets or something."

There was no one in the girls' room.

"Maybe we can see them from up here," Henry suggested. He took the binoculars and looked out from the tower. "Nope, all I see is Sandy Munson driving the Jeep up the hill. Let's go out and see if Jessie and Violet went back to the greenhouse."

"Okay," Benny agreed. "Why are you taking Jessie's hat, Henry?"

"Maybe Watch can catch Jessie's scent and follow the girls."

Benny liked this idea very much. On the way to the greenhouse, the boys took one last look back at the castle. Maybe the girls were playing a game of hide-and-seek with them.

"Henry! Look up at that window." Benny pointed to the rose window over the front door. "It's moving!"

Indeed there seemed to be someone looking out from the center of the round stained glass window where the painted knight was supposed to be.

Henry grabbed Benny's hand and raced back to the door.

"Shucks!" Benny said when they got closer. "I guess it was just somebody going by in that room."

"I guess so," Henry agreed. "Let's ask Carrie about getting into it sometime. There's something strange about that window."

When the boys got to the stables, Watch raced toward them. When he sniffed Jessie's bright red cap, he wagged his tail eagerly.

"Go find Jessie, boy," Henry said.

Watch put his nose to the ground. Then he went right inside the stable and stood under a window. There on a windowsill was a wrapped piece of candy.

"Good boy, Watch!" Benny cried when he saw the candy his sisters had left for him. "This is more fun than following any old map."

It sure was. With another sniff of Jessie's hat, Watch led Henry and Benny to a toolshed. Lo and behold, there was a wrapped candy waiting right up on a shelf next to an old toolbox.

"The girls can't be too far ahead," Henry said. "Watch is a better guide than a map any day."

The boys were sure they would catch up to their sisters very soon. Watch led them to the next stop, a pretty ironwork summer-house with a bench inside.

"Grape!" Henry announced as he unwrapped a purple candy.

"Look, Henry, they even left a dog biscuit for Watch!" Benny said in amazement.

Benny waited while Watch finished his munching and crunching. Then Benny gave him Jessie's hat to sniff again. "I like this treasure hunt!" he told Henry.

Watch ran ahead of the boys. He stopped in front of an old blue door built into the hillside. They had never noticed it before because it was partly hidden by bushes.

Henry turned the doorknob. The door didn't budge.

"They can't have gone in here," Henry told Benny. "The door is locked tight."

"Tell that to Watch," Benny laughed.

"He keeps walking back and forth in front of this door."

The boys pulled and pushed, then turned and twisted the rusted iron doorknob. Nothing happened.

"Watch must be wrong," Benny said.

Henry put Jessie's hat under Watch's nose again. "Find Jessie, boy."

Again Watch paced back and forth in front of the door.

"Let's go back to where we started at the greenhouse," Henry suggested. "Maybe the girls are back by now. Or maybe they went another way when they couldn't get this door open."

This time the boys took the path along the cliff. They looked down to see if their sisters had gone to the lake. When they passed the entrance to the footpath, Watch dashed down the steps.

"Watch! Watch!" Henry called out.

Watch kept right on going.

"We'd better follow him," Henry told Benny.

The boys could hear Watch sniffing ahead

of them. Finally he stopped right in front of the gate to the cave.

"Henry! Benny! Here we are," Jessie cried, peering out when her brothers got close. "We're in here."

Henry pulled at the gate. "What? How did you get in here? It's locked."

"I know it's locked," Jessie began. "Open it with that big key, and we'll tell you about our adventure."

Henry and Benny looked at each other with surprise.

"What key?" Henry asked. "We don't have any key."

Now the girls were surprised.

"Didn't you find the key we left hanging by the blue door? We left it there with a few candies so you would notice it and follow us into that end of the cave. Now we're locked in."

"We didn't notice any candies or any key," Benny said in a shaky voice. He didn't like seeing his sisters behind the locked gate.

Jessie tried not to get nervous. "We put the key back and locked the door behind us.

Then we followed the cave until we got here. Go back and see if the key fell on the ground."

Henry raced off while Benny waited with his sisters. "Is it spooky in there?" he asked in a very small voice.

Violet smiled at Benny. "It is a little spooky. The cave twists and turns a long, long way under the cliff until it stops here. Jessie and I were glad that Carrie gave us flashlights when we went back for the candy. She's the one who told us about the key. It probably opens this gate, too."

Henry came back all out of breath. "The key and the candy are gone!"

"They are?" Jessie asked. "Why, we put the key right back! I know we did. Who could have taken it?"

"Someone must have been watching us, Jessie," Violet said. "Someone who wanted us to get locked in. But who?"

"We'll have to find that out," Henry said. "But first I have to get you free. In the tool shed I found this metal cutter to break the lock. We've all had enough adventure for today."

"That's for sure," Benny agreed.

Henry worked away at the old lock until he was able to pull it apart. As soon as the gate opened, Watch went up to the two girls and licked them over and over.

"There, there, boy, it wasn't so bad," Violet said.

All the same she waited outside while Henry and Benny took a few steps inside the cave to see what it was like.

"We'll have to come back with a bigger flashlight," Henry said. "First I want to find out what happened to that key and who sent us on this wild goose chase with this useless map."

"You mean a dog chase, don't you, Henry?" Benny asked. "Not a goose chase."

Everyone laughed at Benny's good joke.

"Too bad we didn't find any treasures," Jessie said to Benny.

"But we did!" Benny said. "You and Violet were the treasures!"

CHAPTER 7

Benny Solves a Puzzle

"What an adventure!" Benny announced when he came back to the castle.

The children chattered on about their morning while they helped Carrie get lunch. As usual, Benny was starving, which was too bad. Lunch that day was just dibs and dabs of leftovers from the day before.

"Sorry about serving reruns again, Benny," Carrie said. "I thought Sandy would be back with the groceries by now."

"I found one can of tuna fish left," Jessie said when she looked in the almost empty cabinets. "Maybe I can stretch it out."

Carrie looked disgusted. "That Sandy! Where can she be? She promised to be back by lunchtime."

Henry was surprised to hear this. "Wait a minute. At least an hour ago Benny and I saw a red Jeep driving back toward the castle. Wasn't that Sandy?"

"That must have been someone else on the lake road," Carrie said. "It's too bad it wasn't Sandy. I guess we'll have to make do with what food we have."

By the time everyone had sat down to eat, the lunch tasted just fine to the Aldens. Their morning's adventure had made them hungry for anything, even leftovers.

"We're going to start work on the stained glass windows in the towers this afternoon," Carrie announced when lunch was over. "I've got this book of old photos and water-colors that show how the windows looked originally."

Violet studied the pictures of Drummond Castle as it once was. "Do you think someday the castle will really look like this again?"

Carrie gave Violet a smile. "With patience and care, we can do anything. Now let's find Mr. Tooner. Your grandfather mentioned you like drawing and painting, Violet. I think you might be of special help."

Mr. Tooner was halfway up the staircase in the other tower when the Aldens caught up with him. He didn't even turn around when Carrie came up with the Aldens. He just went right on taking down the plywood coverings from the damaged windows.

"Already at work, I see," Carrie said to Mr. Tooner. "Violet is going to sketch the windows from the picture and number the window pieces that are missing. Then we can give her sketches and your measurements to the glassmaker."

"If you like, you can hand things to us, Mr. Tooner," Henry said. "We can help you put back the plywood coverings."

Jessie gathered up old nails scattered around the floor. "These can be used again if we hammer them straight. Can Benny borrow this extra hammer?"

"Humph," was Mr. Tooner's answer.

The children decided this meant yes. Soon Benny was banging away on the nails to make them straight. Henry helped take down the plywood so Mr. Tooner wouldn't have to go up and down his step stool every time. As Mr. Tooner uncovered each window, Violet made sketches to show the missing pieces. Then Jessie labeled them with the measurements.

After each window was done, Benny handed Mr. Tooner nice straight nails to hammer on the coverings again.

"Did I do these right, Mr. Tooner?" Violet asked when she put down her colored pencils.

Mr. Tooner looked at Violet's drawings. His face seemed to brighten. "Why, yes, Miss, yes. That is just the way they should be."

After that, Mr. Tooner didn't seem to mind that the Aldens were there.

"I can see you don't need me," Carrie said. "I'll be downstairs. Maybe Sandy is back by now."

Mr. Tooner and the Aldens labeled every

window along the tower staircase until they got to the top floor.

"Are we going in here?" Henry asked when they came to a locked door. "Carrie says no one goes in that room."

"This room is closed up, but look what I have," Mr. Tooner said. He jiggled some keys in his pocket. The children all wondered the same thing. Did Mr. Tooner have the big key to the blue door?

He didn't. When he held up his key ring, they saw it had only small, ordinary-sized keys on it.

Mr. Tooner opened the door to the mysterious tower room, and they all went inside. The room was cluttered with boxes and old furniture and toys. Most of the windows were plain leaded ones. There was another one hidden under a square of plywood. When Mr. Tooner and Henry pulled down the wood covering, a rainbow of colors filled the room.

"It's hardly damaged at all!" Jessie cried. "Just one or two pieces are missing."

Mr. Tooner showed the children just how

to measure the pieces that needed to be replaced. Violet sketched them and wrote down the measurements. The children, and even Mr. Tooner, hummed and hammered, measured and whistled. When they had finished, the children looked around the room.

"This looks like an old attic," Benny said. "I guess that's why no one comes up here."

"It's too bad," Jessie said. "We like our two little tower rooms on the other side."

This made Henry realize something. "Isn't it strange that this room is only as big as *one* of our rooms? Since the towers are the same size from the outside, they should be the same size on the inside!"

"Or there should be another room," Jessie said, puzzled.

"I'd like to find a secret room," Benny said. He crawled behind the old toys and suits of armor piled up all around. He tried to look behind the bookcase, but realized it was built into the wall.

"This has been used as a storage room ever since Mr. Drummond died," Mr. Tooner said. "Once it was used as a playroom for

some of the servants' children. There's prob-
ably a crawlspace around it, nothing more.
Well, we're finished with these windows.
Let's go downstairs and work on the others."

As Benny left the room, he took one last
look at the suit of armor standing in the corner of the room. He knew it was impossible,
but he was almost certain he'd seen it move.
He hurried to catch up with the others.

"Listen," Violet whispered to Jessie as
they followed Mr. Tooner down the tower
stairs. "Mr. Tooner is humming that same
fiddle tune we heard."

Mr. Tooner's humming carried clearly up
the stone staircase.

"You're right," Jessie said. "But I don't
think it has anything to do with the missing
violin. He's too nice to be mixed up with
that."

Henry overheard the girls. "I bet Mr.
Tooner sometimes hears that same music,
and it just got into his head. He probably
doesn't even realize where that tune came
from!"

"Well, anyway I'm glad he's humming instead of being grouchy like before," Violet agreed.

The children stopped whispering when they caught up with Mr. Tooner. He waved them down a hall on the second floor toward the front of the castle.

"Where to now, Mr. Tooner?" Henry shifted the step stool from one shoulder to another.

"Another secret room?" Benny joked.

For the first time, the children saw Mr. Tooner smile a real smile. His blue eyes twinkled.

"You guessed right, my boy," Mr. Tooner said to Benny. "Now follow me. Henry, you can put down that ladder. You girls can leave the toolbox and papers in the hall. Nothing needs fixing in here."

With that, Mr. Tooner pulled out his key ring again. He opened a door to another small room filled with soft colored light.

"It's the room with the round stained glass window over the front door!" Violet cried.

"Yes, indeed," Mr. Tooner said. "Mr.

Drummond used to spend a lot of time here. He had this room and that window specially designed."

Mr. Tooner went over to the window and clicked two latches. Out fell the central piece of stained glass. The children gasped.

"Don't worry. It's not broken," Mr. Tooner said with a very nice smile. "Here Benny, hold this piece over your face."

Benny carefully took the painted piece of the knight's face. It fit right over his own! Benny knew just what to do next. He went over to the empty space and put his own face in the window. It fit almost perfectly.

"I can see everything from up here!" he cried.

"And so could Mr. Drummond," Mr. Tooner explained. "He designed the removable glass so he could see who came to the door ahead of time. Then he would decide if he wanted to meet with a visitor or not."

Mr. Tooner slapped his knee. "I sometimes do the same. Half the time people who come to the door are just a plain bother. If

I don't like 'em, I don't answer the door."

"You must have liked us, Mr. Tooner," Violet said. "I saw a face the day we arrived at Drummond Castle. Remember? You were the one who answered the door."

Mr. Tooner shook his head. "I answered the door, but I haven't been in this room for weeks. Too much work to do."

"But . . . but, someone was here," Violet said. "Now that I know this is a lookout, I'm sure someone was watching us the day we drove up."

"What about this morning?" Henry asked Mr. Tooner. "Benny and I are sure someone was up here. But when we got close, the person moved away."

"Can't be, my boy, can't be," Mr. Tooner told Henry. "Even Mrs. Bell doesn't have a key. She thinks it's my private storage room and doesn't bother me about it."

The children were completely confused. They couldn't say for sure that they had seen a face in the funny window. But they certainly thought they had.

CHAPTER 8

Mysterious Music

When the children came downstairs to help with dinner, Carrie was on the phone.

"Just wait there," Carrie said, disgusted. "I can't imagine why you ran out of gas. There was enough in the tank for at least one trip to town. Never mind. I'll send someone for you right away."

"What is it, Caroline?" Mr. Alden asked when he saw how upset his old friend was.

Carrie shook her head. "It's Sandy, of course. Who else would have forgotten to fill the gas tank? What I can't figure out is why she ran out of gas at all. The tank was low, but she should have been able to make it to town. And why is she calling so late when she left this morning?"

"There, there," Mr. Alden said. "Henry and I will go for her. Now where was Miss Munson calling from?"

"From a pay phone where the lake road and the highway meet," Carrie answered.

After Mr. Alden and Henry left, Benny and Violet began to set the table. Jessie checked the pantry, then the refrigerator.

"I guess we'll have to wait for Sandy to get back with the groceries," Jessie said. "We can figure out what to make for dinner when we see what she bought."

Carrie twisted a dish cloth she had in her hands. "Sandy is so unreliable. I wish the Drummond Foundation had let me interview her myself. What good is it to know all about the castle and not be dependable?"

A half hour later, when it was dinnertime, Henry and Mr. Alden walked in the door, with Sandy Munson right behind.

"Hello, Sandy," Carrie said without a smile. "If we all help unload the groceries from the Jeep, we can get dinner on the table."

"But there's nothing to unload," Mr. Alden told Carrie. "Didn't Miss Munson tell you she ran out of gas *before* she ever got to town?"

Sandy looked down at the floor. "I . . . I'll go back to town in the morning, Carrie. I'm sorry. I guess I was lower on gas than you thought. Somebody can have my portion of whatever you have for dinner."

"That won't be much, Sandy," Carrie said. "We have very little food. I had hoped to restock today." Carrie looked around the kitchen at all her hungry helpers. "We can discuss this in the morning."

Jessie found some eggs to make omelets. Violet sprinkled drops of water on the breakfast rolls to freshen them up before reheating them.

"We can make custard with the rest of this milk and the eggs," Benny suggested. "Our housekeeper, Mrs. MacGregor, showed me how. It's easy!"

"I'll help you, Benny," Sandy offered. She looked ashamed. For a change she tried to cheer up the children instead of scolding them. "There are some custard molds up in this cabinet. They have a pretty snowflake pattern on the bottom. I used to make custard with my mother."

"How did you know about the custard molds with the snowflake patterns?" Carrie asked.

When Sandy heard this she dropped the tin molds on the floor. "I . . . well . . . the other day I was looking for . . . uh . . . something else in that cabinet. They're like the ones I had when I was a little girl."

The children looked at Sandy closely when she rinsed off the custard tins. This wasn't the first time she seemed to know more than a newcomer would about some of the things in Drummond Castle. Had she been here before?

Sandy went about helping Benny without saying much. She didn't speak at all during the skimpy dinner everyone ate. Right afterwards she excused herself and went upstairs. She didn't even wait for the custard to finish baking. "I'll be in my room all night," Sandy said. "I'm sorry about today."

"I guess I'll have to go grocery shopping with her tomorrow unless we all want to go on a diet!" Carrie said.

"I don't!" Benny said, as he spooned up the last of the very good custard.

Carrie ruffled Benny's hair. "Well you won't have to. Now why don't you children run up to your rooms and relax? On your way up, just knock on Sandy's door. Tell her we'll leave for town at eight sharp."

"Okay," the children said as they went upstairs.

There was no light coming from under Sandy's door when Jessie gave a knock.

"That's odd. She doesn't seem to be there," Jessie said.

"I guess we'd better find her if we want to eat tomorrow, right Ben?" Henry joked.

"Then let's look for her," Benny said.

The children checked some of the other rooms near Sandy's. All of them were dark or locked.

"Let's try the other wing," Jessie suggested. "You never know where Sandy will show up."

The children got their flashlights and took the long passageway that led to the other side of the castle. The hall was dark and cold, and so were the rooms off of it. None of them had been used for many years. Benny and Violet held hands tightly. Suddenly, the children heard faraway notes of sweet violin music.

Violet hummed softly. She whispered to Benny. "I know this is strange, but when I hear that tune, I'm not as scared."

But a moment later all the children were scared. When they reached the spiral staircase to the second tower, they saw a light moving up the stairs. The children stood at the bottom looking up the corkscrew turns. At each turn the light went higher and higher. Finally it disappeared at the top.

"Let's go up," Henry said. "Follow me."

The children crept up the stairs without making a sound. The staircase was just like the one to their own room in the other tower.

They didn't need much light. They held on to the twisted iron railing and made their way up, step by step.

When they reached the landing, they expected anything but what they saw.

Nothing — except a locked door.

There was no one at the top of the stairs.

"How can that be?" Jessie asked. "The door is locked. The light that was here is gone."

Henry jiggled the doorknob.

"It's no use," he said. He banged on the door. "Hello! Hello! Is anyone there?"

No one answered.

"Beats me," Henry said, tapping his forehead in amazement. "Let's see if we can get Mr. Tooner to let us in. He has the key."

Going down was less scary. The children turned on their flashlights. They didn't whisper, and they didn't tiptoe. It didn't matter whether anyone heard them now.

The children followed a path outside that ran along the cliff to Mr. Tooner's house. They thought they heard violin music again, but it was hard to tell with the strong wind blowing across the lake.

"Do you think Mr. Tooner will mind our visit?" Violet asked.

Henry looked thoughtful. "I think he would want to know if anyone is up in the tower who shouldn't be.

The path ended at a small stone house. The children peeked in the window. Mr. Tooner was putting away a music stand.

Henry rang the doorbell. Mr. Tooner came to the window and looked out. He made a face and began to close the shutters. Then he realized the Aldens were at the door.

Although Mr. Tooner didn't smile, he didn't look mad anymore either. "Is there any trouble?" he asked the children.

Violet stepped up to the door. She had a feeling Mr. Tooner liked her. "We think somebody's up in the tower room. We followed somebody all the way up the stairs, but the door was locked when we got there."

"Turn around! Look up there!" Mr. Tooner pointed up at the tower. "By golly, there is someone up there. A light is on."

Before they knew it, the Aldens were following Mr. Tooner to a small door at the back of his house. It opened into a cave passageway.

"Does this cave lead to the castle?" Jessie asked.

"See for yourself," Mr. Tooner said. He turned on two small overhead lights that brightened the passageway.

"Neat!" Benny said. "You can go back and forth to the castle without going outside."

The passageway was quite short. Soon the children were following Mr. Tooner up the tower stairs. At the top, he pulled out his key ring and unlocked the door.

There was no electricity in this part of the castle. The children and Mr. Tooner used their flashlights to search the cluttered room.

"Whoever was here must be gone by now," Henry said. "Sorry to bother you with this, Mr. Tooner."

"That's all right, my boy. I saw that light, too," Mr. Tooner said. "Somebody must have made a copy of my keys, that's all I can think."

"Come on — let's go," Jessie said. "I just want to see if I can see the moon through the chimney," Benny answered, standing in the fireplace and looking up. "But there's no chimney in this funny fireplace. Whoops — "

The other children heard a thud and ran over to see what had happened to Benny. But he had disappeared!

Then they heard his voice, from the other side of the wall. "This is a fake fireplace! If you push it, there's another room!" Benny yelled. "Lean hard, like I did, and it will turn around."

The children and Mr. Tooner did just that. They managed to push themselves into a moonlit room the same size as the one they had just been in. Like the other room, this one was filled with old furniture, books, and toys. Mr. Tooner and the Aldens poked around as best they could in the dim light. Suddenly, while their backs were turned,

they heard the creaking of the revolving wall.

"Oh no!" Jessie cried out. "Whoever was in here just got out."

Everyone pushed at the movable wall, and it revolved again. They were back on the other side. But they were too late. The mysterious person had disappeared.

"Guess I'll lock up. Not that it does much good if somebody's got the key." Mr. Tooner sounded upset. "I only hope whoever copied this key didn't copy any others. Mr. Drummond trusted me to keep an eye on things, and that's what I've done. But now . . ."

Violet patted Mr. Tooner's hand. "It'll be okay. You did a good job. We can help you find whoever it is who got in here."

Everyone wanted to cheer up the old man. "We'll help you put in some new locks," Henry said. "We're handy with tools."

"A secret room, a secret room," Mr. Tooner repeated. "I thought I knew every corner of this castle."

"There, there," Violet said. "Tomorrow we'll try to figure out who really does know every corner of this castle."

CHAPTER 9

Vanished into Thin Air

Carrie Bell was in a hurry. "I wish I didn't have to go to town with Sandy," she told the Alden children. "I'd much rather poke around the secret room this morning. I guess I'll have to wait a bit," she said with a sigh. "Imagine! A whole roomful of treasures we didn't even know about!"

"What didn't we know about?" Sandy asked when she came in and overheard Carrie.

Benny's face lit up. "We found a secret room last night with Mr. Tooner. It's full of

95

toys and armor and treasures. Carrie said we could go up there this morning."

This seemed to upset Sandy. "Alone?"

"I trust these children with anything in the castle," Carrie explained. "So does Mr. Tooner. Before he went out for the day with Mr. Alden, he gave me his keys. He trusts the children with them, and so do I."

"Well, shouldn't I stay behind and supervise them at least?" Sandy asked.

Carrie handed Sandy the grocery list. "First things first. We simply must get supplies and groceries this morning. The sooner we get to town, the sooner we can help the children."

This didn't stop Sandy. "Well maybe the children should come with us," she said to Carrie. "We could split up the errands and get them done faster."

Carrie shook her head. "That's just what Tom Brady suggested this morning. He wanted to take them along to visit some antique dealers. I had to tell him the same thing. Mr. Tooner and I feel fine about leaving the Aldens here alone until we all get back. That's really final, Sandy."

"I guess now we're kings of the castle, right Benny?" Henry joked after Carrie and Sandy finally left. "What do you say we put on some armor and go jousting!"

"What's jousting?" Benny asked.

Violet explained. "Jousting is a horseback-riding sport that knights played in the olden days, Benny. I read about it in my King Arthur book. Sometimes this castle reminds me of those times."

"Especially the tower," Benny said. "Can we go up there now?"

"Sure Ben," Henry said. "But let's clear up the table first, okay? Even knights need clean dishes."

The children carried the breakfast dishes to the sink. When Benny got to Tom's place at the table he noticed something. "Isn't this Tom's notebook?"

"It is," Jessie said. "We can drop it off at his office when we finish in here."

Once the children had tidied up every-thing, they stopped off at the room Tom Brady used as an office.

"Should we leave the notebook in front of the door?" Benny asked. "Grandfather says we shouldn't go into someone's room unless the person is there."

Jessie shook her head. "This time we have to, Benny. The hall is so dark I'm afraid someone might trip over the notebook. Let's put it on Tom's desk with a note saying that we found it."

The children opened the door to the jumbled office. For someone who was so careful about old things, Tom Brady was careless about everything else. His wastebasket was overflowing with papers. Several half-empty mugs of cold tea were still on the desk. There wasn't an inch of empty space to put down the notebook.

Jessie tried to make some room on the desk to write Tom a note. She moved over several books and picked up some bunched-up balls of paper.

"Wait a minute!" she cried. "Look at these!" She held up two colored cellophane candy wrappers. "Aren't these the wrappers from the candy Violet and I hid yesterday?"

Benny found one or two other wrappers in the wastebasket. "Lemon, cherry."

"Lime and grape," Violet finished. "Those are exactly the same flavors Jessie and I hid by the blue door because we knew they were your favorites!"

"The ones that were missing along with the key!" Henry realized. "Do you think Tom took them, Jessie?"

Jessie didn't answer. She ran out of the room and came back a few minutes later. She waved a piece of notebook paper at her brothers and sister.

"Look at this! It's the map!" She laid the paper next to Tom's notebook. "I can't say for sure that the candy wrappers came from the candy we hid. But this map exactly matches the paper in Tom's notebook."

"So does the handwriting," Violet added.

"It *is* the same," Benny said proudly. Even though he hadn't been reading for long, he was sure of that.

The children looked at each other. What was going on with Tom Brady?

Jessie made up her mind about something.

"Let's show the map to Tom. Maybe there's a good reason he drew it. It could be a set of directions he wrote up for someone, then put in that book by mistake. He might be glad to get it back."

Henry agreed. "Jessie's right. Let's see what Tom has to say when we show him what we found."

"Aw, shucks," Benny said. "I thought we solved a mystery."

"Sorry, Benny, not just yet," Jessie said with a laugh. "Now let's get up to the secret room. Maybe there's a mystery to solve up there."

"I sure hope so," Benny said as he raced ahead up the tower stairs.

When they got to the top, the children waited for Henry to open the door with Mr. Tooner's keys.

"Here we are," Henry said.

Benny paid no attention to all the treasures in the room. "Can we go to the secret room first, Henry?"

Henry laughed. "Why not? Carrie said we could go anywhere in the castle today. We might as well start sorting things out in there as well as in here."

Benny got right inside the fake fireplace. He leaned against it just the way he had the day before. Nothing happened. He turned around then pushed so hard he grunted. "This wall is stuck!"

"Here, Benny. You give a push on the bottom, while I push hard on top," Henry said.

But try as they might, the boys couldn't get the fireplace to turn. Then Benny noticed something. Right at his eye level, there was a keyhole. He looked in.

Just a few feet inside was Tom Brady! And in Tom's hand was a violin. "Tom?" Benny called through the wall.

Suddenly the wall panel gave way and the Aldens pushed through into the secret room. There was Tom Brady — but his hands were empty.

"I was wondering when you children would find me," Tom said with a laugh. "This was a good game of hide-and-seek, wasn't it?"

The children were confused. One minute Tom had been trying to keep them out of the secret room. Now he was telling them he had been playing a game!

"Carrie said you left to meet some antique dealers this morning," Jessie said. "Why are you here instead?" Now that she was facing Tom, Jessie wasn't so sure it was the right time to mention the notebook. She decided to wait.

"Umm . . . well, yes, I was going to do just that but . . . uh, first I had to get something up here," Tom said without looking at Jessie.

"Like a violin!" Benny said. "I saw you holding a violin when I peeked in the keyhole. Is it the famous one?" Benny asked as he scooted behind Tom.

"What violin?" Tom asked. "There are many musical instruments in this house. We all know William Drummond collected quite a few of them."

By this time Benny had opened the doors of an old cabinet. "Like this one?" he cried when he spotted the neck of a violin.

Tom Brady whirled around. "Don't touch that!" he yelled at Benny. "It's priceless."

Jessie stared at Tom with her steady brown eyes. "How do you know that violin is priceless?"

"Well, everything up here is priceless until we catalogue it and get estimates from antique dealers," he said. "That's all I meant. We must get experts in here."

This did not stop Jessie Alden. "You said *you* were an expert when we first came here. Remember? You said you didn't want us touching anything or working with you."

"True, true," Tom looked nervously around the room. "We do have to go about things in a certain way. I can't have people poking around all over the castle. These valuable things must be handled with care."

"Then why did you just shove the violin in this cabinet?" Benny asked. "Violet always puts hers carefully away in its case.

Tom took the violin from the cabinet. He cradled it in his arms as if to protect it. "How did I have any way of knowing who was at the door? Many dealers have been after the

violin for years, coming to the castle and wanting to look around."

Violet stepped forward. "Then this is the Stradivarius, isn't it? Look how beautiful it is!"

Tom pulled a violin case out from behind a bookcase. "I won't know until I study it and compare it to photos of other violins of this type. Why, I can do that this afternoon." He carefully laid the violin in its case and snapped the lock shut before the children could get a closer look.

"Why don't we let Carrie decide what to do about this violin and some of the other things in here?" Henry asked. "After all she's part of the restoration group at the castle, too."

Tom didn't answer right away. But when he did, his whole mood had changed. He smiled at Henry and the other children. "You're quite right, quite right, young fellow. This will be a feather in Carrie's cap if the violin is the missing one. I think we should all surprise her at dinner tonight. That will give me time to look up my notes and find out if this is the Drummond Stradivarius."

"Are you going to look in your notebook?" Benny asked.

Jessie grabbed Benny's hand before Tom had a chance to answer. "Come on, Benny. Let's go downstairs and wait for Carrie. I think Tom has a good plan. We can surprise Carrie tonight if the violin is the one we've all been looking for."

Benny didn't like this idea one bit. Why did Jessie want to go along with Tom's plan? It didn't make sense.

"Benny and I have a few things to do downstairs," Jessie told Henry and Violet. "Maybe you can stay here and help Tom organize some of these things until we get back."

Henry and Violet had a feeling Jessie had a plan of her own. What was it?

CHAPTER 10

One Last Song

Benny and Jessie were glad when everyone came back early. From the window they could see their grandfather and Mr. Tooner unloading some bushes to plant along the drive. They heard Carrie drive the Jeep up to the kitchen entrance.

Benny looked up at Jessie. She would make everything turn out right. But he was mixed up. "Why did we let Tom keep that violin?" he asked his sister. "Isn't it the famous one?"

"Tom does have the famous violin,

Benny," Jessie said. "I am sure of it. That's why I need you to help me with my plan. We have to make sure the violin doesn't leave Drummond Castle until the police get here."

Benny's big brown eyes got even bigger. "The police are coming?"

Jessie nodded. "They will be when I get Grandfather away from Mr. Tooner and Carrie away from Sandy, so Grandfather and Carrie can call the police. I'm still not sure who knows about the violin."

"Not Mr. Tooner!" Benny whispered. "I think he's nice."

Jessie smiled. "I think so too. But I can't understand why we found him in Grand-father's room and why he didn't seem to want us at Drummond Castle." Jessie stopped talk-ing. A sad look passed over her face. "We know he plays the violin. I'm afraid that makes him a suspect."

This made Benny sad, too. "Grandfather likes Mr. Tooner. He wouldn't like someone who would take things."

"I know," Jessie said. "That's why we have to find out more about Tom. Then maybe we can figure out Mr. Tooner."

"And Sandy!" Benny said. "Maybe she and Tom are friends, and they took the violin together."

"That is just what we have to find out. Now let's find Grandfather, then Carrie."

Jessie took Benny by the hand. They walked out to the grounds to see Mr. Alden.

"Well, hello, you two," Mr. Alden said. "Have you found that violin yet?" he joked.

"We found lots of things up in the other tower," Benny answered truthfully.

While Benny chatted with Mr. Alden, Jessie studied Mr. Tooner's face. He seemed curious about what Benny was saying, not angry like Tom.

"Grandfather, could you come in and talk to Carrie now that she's back?" Jessie asked.

As soon as they were inside the castle, Jessie and Benny told their grandfather that Tom had found the Stradivarius.

"Then we must call the police right away," Mr. Alden agreed. "I will tell Caroline what has happened."

"Please be careful not to tell her in front

of Sandy," Jessie reminded her grandfather. "We don't know if she and Tom are trying to steal the violin together."

As planned, Mr. Alden went down to get Carrie. He was going to tell Sandy the children needed her to help up in the secret room of the tower.

Jessie and Benny climbed the tower stairs. Henry and Violet were already busy at work. Tom had the violin case right by his side as he took notes on a piece of paper. Every few minutes he walked over to the window to look out. He seemed restless, but not too restless to keep a close watch on the violin case.

Jessie knew she had to keep Tom away from the tower windows. She didn't want him to see the police pull up. She found some beautiful old books in one of the bookcases.

"Tom, could you look through these books to see whether they are valuable?" Jessie asked. "If they're not, then maybe we can donate them to the library."

Tom didn't seem to be interested, but this didn't stop Jessie. "You know, we're leaving in a couple of days. We really should decide about these right away."

"All right, all right," Tom said. He walked over to the bookcase in the corner, away from the windows. He kept the violin with him.

For someone who was an expert on rare books, Tom handled the old fairy tales roughly. He opened and shut the delicate covers as if these were ordinary books.

This upset Violet. She had a feeling Jessie wanted Tom to stay busy. She went over to the bookcase, too. "I could read off the titles of the books and the names of the authors and illustrators," she suggested to Tom. "Then you could write down the information. That would take less time."

"Fine, fine," Tom said impatiently.

Violet and Tom had just settled down to do this when Sandy came into the secret room.

"What are you doing here?" she asked Tom. "This is just an old playroom. Shouldn't you be working downstairs where the real antiques are?"

Jessie and Benny looked at each other. If

Tom and Sandy were a team, they didn't act like one. Sandy seemed to want Tom out of the room.

"Those are my fairy tales," she said when she saw a pile of books next to Tom. "I want to keep them."

"Your fairy tales?" Tom cried. "What are you talking about?"

Sandy looked like she was about to cry. She ran to the corner and grabbed an armful of the books. She opened several of them to the title pages. "See, there. It says: 'Sandra Munson' there and there."

"So you *are* the same Sandy?" a man's voice said.

The children turned around to see Mr. Tooner standing in the doorway.

"Yes," Sandy said softly, "I am."

"I thought so," Mr. Tooner said with a smile. Then he turned to the children and explained. "Sandy was the last child to ever live in Drummond Castle. Mr. Drummond hired her mother as a cook, and she and Sandy both lived here many years ago."

"Mr. Drummond was old and kind,"

Sandy said. "He let me use these rooms as my bedroom and playroom. He gave me these books and toys that had belonged to his children. I didn't think Mr. Tooner would recognize me," Sandy said. "I was only ten years old when we left. My mother found a job as a chef at a big hotel, so we moved there. But I always wanted to come back to Drummond Castle where I'd been so happy. I wanted to sit and look out of the tower, and find my old books and toys again."

Mr. Tooner patted Sandy's hand. "Well, young lady, why didn't you tell anyone who you were? Mrs. Bell, why she would have put out the welcome mat for you."

"Well, I wasn't sure," Sandy said. "And I wanted so much to come back — I couldn't take the chance on being turned away. When I saw the ad for an assistant, I decided to tell the Drummond Foundation that I had researched everything about the castle. That's what made them hire me. And once I'd made up that story, I didn't want anyone to find out I'd lied about who I really was — or why I wanted the job."

"My, my," Mr. Tooner said quietly. "From the first day I had a feeling I had seen you before. But you know, I'm an old fellow now, and my memory's not so good. I wasn't sure. Besides, a man like me is set in his ways. Can't say that I liked people coming in here and upsetting everything."

This made Sandy laugh just a little. "That's just what I did, didn't I? Upset everything. I was so nervous all the time, I kept making mistakes."

"Is this yours?" Benny said. He pulled out the charm bracelet he had found and forgotten to give to Sandy.

"I found it under a dust sheet on a chair in the great hall," Violet told Sandy. "How did it get there?"

Sandy hung her head down. She started crying again. "I followed you children around. I was afraid that somehow you would figure out who I was. The day you were going to work in the great hall, I remembered that some of my old books were in there, and they had my name written inside. I went to hide them, but I didn't have enough time. I hid under the dust sheet when you came in."

"That was a good hiding place," Benny said. "And a scary one."

Everyone laughed but Tom. He hadn't said a word since Sandy started talking.

"I was just so happy to be here, and I didn't want to get caught in a silly lie. But you children were all over the place," Sandy explained. "The day I thought you were going on a treasure hunt, I was afraid of what you might find. I only pretended to drive to town, but I came back and parked in the woods and watched you from the tower."

"And from the stained glass window?" Henry asked. "Benny and I thought we saw someone looking at us from the window over the front door."

Sandy dried her tears. She wasn't crying now. She just looked plain confused. "What stained glass window?"

"The one with the knight's face in the middle that you can take out to see who's coming and going," Violet explained. "Wasn't that you?"

The Aldens could see Sandy Munson had no idea what they were talking about.

Tom Brady suddenly stood up. "Well, this story doesn't sound like it's ever going to end. I have work to do. In fact, I have an appointment with a dealer in half an hour. So if you'll all excuse me."

Tom made a move toward the door. He didn't get that far because Henry and Jessie blocked his way.

"You will have to cancel that appointment," Henry told Tom in a clear, strong voice. "Tell the dealer you do not have a violin to sell."

"That violin belongs to Drummond Castle," Jessie added.

Tom clutched the violin case to his chest like a baby. "It belongs to the Drummond family, not Drummond Castle. And I'm the last of the Drummonds. My mother was Mr. Drummond's niece, and that violin was supposed to be left to me. Then old Drummond got it into his head to turn this wreck of a place into a museum and put a priceless violin on display! On display, can you imagine?"

"You're a Drummond?" Henry asked.

"Yes," said Tom.

"Well," Jessie said. "Drummond Castle is not a wreck. It's a beautiful place that your great-uncle wanted other people to share."

Violet spoke up too. "He wanted to share the violin, too, so many people could admire it. Please give it back."

Tom Brady did nothing of the kind. "What a bunch of kids want with a priceless instrument, I can't figure out. But I knew I had to find it before you did. I tried to keep an eye on you from that stained glass window. I even hid in that suit of armor and watched you. I sent you on a wild goose chase with that treasure map just to keep you out of the way! And you're still trying to ruin my plans!"

"I bet you tried to get us lost in the cave," Benny added. "But we didn't stay lost."

Tom Brady was furious. In one last burst of energy, he shoved his way past Jessie and Henry and raced out the door toward the stairs. The children, Sandy, and Mr. Tooner followed behind.

"Look, I see some other hands on the railing — and they're coming up!" Benny cried out.

Grandfather was right about Benny Alden's sharp eyes. The stairs were crowded with people coming up and people going down. Soon there was a traffic jam in the middle. Grandfather, Carrie, and two police officers were on the lower stairs. Tom Brady was in the middle. Everyone else blocked Tom from the upper stairs.

"Hand over that violin," one of the police officers said to Tom. "There's no way down, and no way up. So just give it to us."

Tom lost some of his hard, angry look. "I want to look at it one more time."

"Let's all go downstairs and straighten this out," the other officer said.

Everyone walked down the tower stairs quietly. At the bottom, Tom handed over the violin. "Take it. But for heavens' sake, don't carry it like a sack of potatoes. That is a priceless instrument."

The policeman opened the case. The violin gleamed in the soft light.

"Can I at least look at it one last time?" Tom asked.

The Aldens tried not to feel sorry for him.

"I don't know the difference between this and a guitar," one of the police officers said.

"May I show you the difference?" Mr. Tooner asked the two officers.

Carrie stepped forward. "Please, give it to Mr. Tooner."

Mr. Tooner picked up the precious instrument. He played a squawky note or two to tune it up. Then he slid the bow across the strings. The sweet notes of "Redbird" floated through the castle.

Before the tune was over, he handed the violin to Violet, "You finish it," he said.

Violet carefully picked up the violin and completed the lovely song. When she had finished, she gave the violin back to Mr. Tooner.

"We heard you playing 'Redbird,' " she said shyly, "but we never actually saw you."

Mr. Tooner carefully laid the violin in its case. "Many years ago, Mr. Drummond taught me to play. Nothing fancy. All I ever

knew were country tunes. I have my own fiddle — nothing valuable like this beauty, but I can squeak out a note or two."

"Indeed you can," Carrie said. "According to Mr. Drummond's will, the Stradivarius is to go on display at the museum to inspire musicians."

After the police left with Tom, everyone stood in the great hall. They wondered what to do next.

"It's too quiet," Benny complained.

"What we need is some music," Mr. Tooner said. He picked up the Stradivarius, not like a sack of potatoes, but like the priceless violin it was. "I always dreamed of playing this again. That's why I kept looking for it. That's what I was doing the day you children found me in your grandfather's room."

Mr. Tooner tucked the violin under his chin. He drew the bow back and forth, one, two, three. Out came the notes of a lively jig. Just as in the old days, Drummond Castle was filled with music and the sound of dancing feet again.

GERTRUDE CHANDLER WARNER discovered when she was teaching that many readers who like an exciting story could find no books that were both easy and fun to read. She decided to try to meet this need, and her first book, *The Boxcar Children*, quickly proved she had succeeded.

Miss Warner drew on her own experiences to write each mystery. As a child she spent hours watching trains go by on the tracks opposite her family home. She often dreamed about what it would be like to set up housekeeping in a caboose or freight car — the situation the Alden children find themselves in.

When Miss Warner received requests for more adventures involving Henry, Jessie, Violet, and Benny Alden, she began additional stories. In each, she chose a special setting and introduced unusual or eccentric characters who liked the unpredictable.

While the mystery element is central to each of Miss Warner's books, she never thought of them as strictly juvenile mysteries. She liked to stress the Aldens' independence and resourcefulness and their solid New England devotion to using up and making do. The Aldens go about most of their adventures with as little adult supervision as possible — something else that delights young readers.

Miss Warner lived in Putnam, Connecticut, until her death in 1979. During her lifetime, she received hundreds of letters from girls and boys telling her how much they liked her books.